For my mother and for Mauri

Copyright © 2019 by Eva Eland

All rights reserved. Published in the United
States by Random House Children's Books,
a division of Penguin Random House LLC, New
York. Published simultaneously in the United
Kingdom by Penguin Random House UK, London,
in 2019.

Random House and the colophon are registered
trademarks of Penguin Random House LLC.

Visit us on the Web!
rhcbooks.com

Educators and librarians, for a variety of teaching tools, visit us at
RHTeachersLibrarians.com

Library of Congress Cataloging-in-Publication Data is available
upon request.

ISBN 978-0-525-70718-9 (trade) — ISBN 978-0-525-70719-6 (ebook)

MANUFACTURED IN MALAYSIA

10 9 8 7 6 5 4 3 2 1

First American Edition

Eva Eland

WHEN SADNESS IS AT YOUR DOOR

Random House 🏠 New York

Sometimes Sadness
arrives unexpectedly.

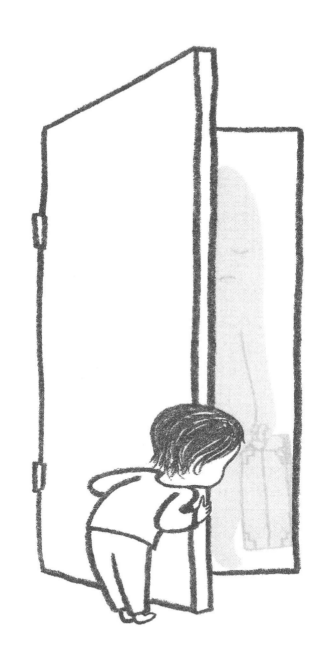

It follows you around...

...and sits so
close to you,
you can hardly
breathe.

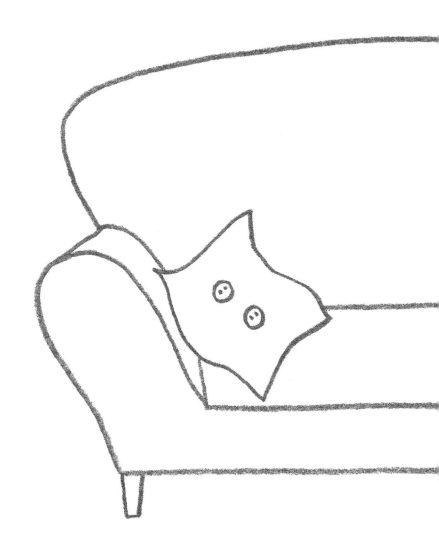

You can try to hide it.

But it feels like you've
become Sadness yourself.

Try not to be afraid
of Sadness.
Give it a name.

hello

Listen to it. Ask where it comes
from and what it needs.

If you don't understand
each other, just sit together
and be quiet for a while.

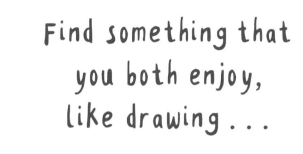

Find something that
you both enjoy,
like drawing . . .

listening to music . . .

or drinking hot
chocolate.

Maybe Sadness doesn't like to stay inside.

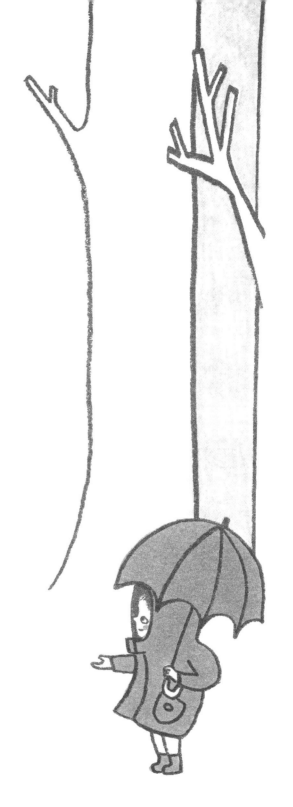

Try letting it out sometimes.

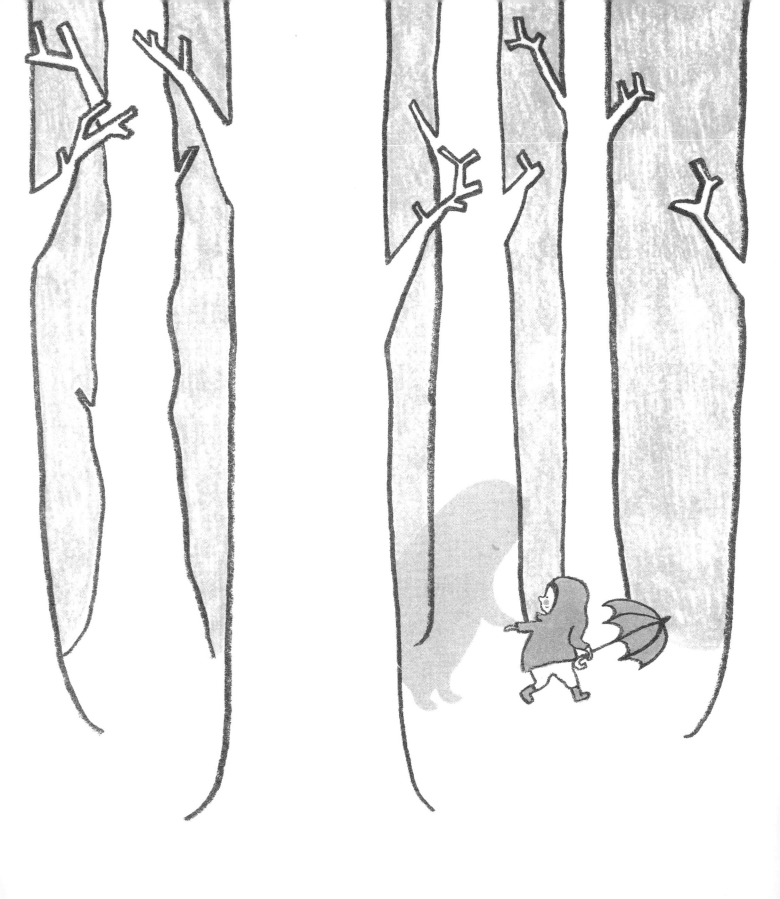

Go for a walk
through the trees.

You can listen to
their sounds together.

Maybe all it wants to know
is that it is welcome.

And to sleep, knowing
it is not alone.

When you wake up,
it might be gone.

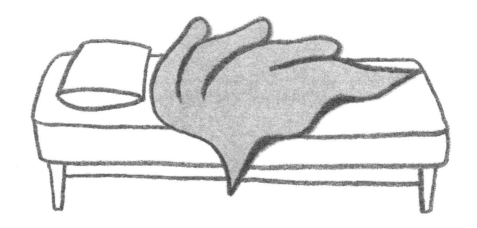

Don't worry—today is a new day.